Adapted by Helena Mayer from the episodes "Flint Sparks the Fire!" and "The Fleeing Tower of Sunyshore!"

The Battle for Sunyshore Tower

SCHOLASTIC INC.

NEW YORK   TORONTO   LONDON   AUCKLAND

SYDNEY   MEXICO CITY   NEW DELHI   HONG KONG

ISBN 978-0-545-28436-3

Published by Scholastic Inc.
SCHOLASTIC and associated logos are trademarks and/or registered trademarks of Scholastic Inc.

12 11 10 9 8 7 6 5 4 3 2 1   11 12 13 14 15/0

Designed by Henry Ng
Printed in the U.S.A.   40
First printing, March 2011

Chapter 1

Sunyshore City gleamed like a diamond in the sun. Shining glass towers scraped the clear sky. Moving sidewalks carried people and Pokémon past leafy green trees. A shimmering blue lagoon stretched as far as the eye could see.

Ash and his friends had been traveling through the Sinnoh region for a long time. They had seen many strange, wondrous, and beautiful things.

But they had never seen anything like this.

Standing at the edge of the city, Dawn gaped at the rainbow-colored buildings. Brock gazed at the exotic Pokémon crowding the streets. But Ash only had eyes for one thing: the Sunyshore Gym.

"I can't *wait* to win the Gym battle and get ahold of my eighth badge!" he said. Pikachu agreed. The little yellow Electric-type Pokémon was eager to show its stuff.

"I wouldn't get overly confident," Dawn warned them. "The Sunyshore Gym Leader's name is Volkner, and I've heard he's tough to beat."

"Yeah." Brock checked his guidebook and frowned. "It says here as the Gym Leader, he's never been defeated. And word on the street is he's the strongest Gym Leader in all of Sinnoh!"

"Ah, big deal," Ash said. He knew his Pokémon were tough enough to take on *anyone*. "The stronger my opponent is, the more fired up I get." He clenched his fist. This battle was going to be a tough one. But that was the way Ash liked it. "Undefeated or not, *I'm* gonna defeat that Gym Leader and get my eighth badge!"

Dawn smiled at her friend. He never walked away from a challenge. It was one of the things that made him such a great Pokémon Trainer.

Suddenly, she caught sight of a huge glass tower. It loomed over the rest of the city.

"Hey, that must be the Sunyshore Tower!" Dawn said.

Brock was excited. "The Sunyshore Gym is near there."

"All right!" Ash cried. "You ready, Pikachu?"

Pikachu cheered. It was as ready as it had ever been.

Pikachu and its friends headed in the direction of the Gym and never looked back.

But maybe they should have.

Because as soon as they were gone, the bushes began to rustle. A moment later, three heads popped out.

It was Team Rocket! And they had heard *everything*.

"So the twerp's here to challenge the Gym for

the win," Meowth said. The crafty Normal-type Pokémon was already hatching a plan.

James grinned. "Perfect time to be on the take —"

"For Pikachu's sake!" Jessie agreed.

Team Rocket pumped their fists in the air. "Yes!" they cheered together. "Great moments we'll make!"

Meowth snickered. He was determined that this time, Team Rocket would finally take down those twerps.

Once and for all.

Chapter 2

"Whoa!" Ash's eyes widened as they reached the Gym. It was a round, silver building with a sparkling glass roof. The only way in was through large steel double doors. And they were shut tight.

"*Welcome.*" The voice came out of nowhere. It was metallic and flat, like the building itself had spoken.

Ash and his friends looked around to see who had greeted them. But no one was there.

"*May I help you?*" the voice asked.

Ash realized there was a speaker over the double doors.

"You bet!" he said loudly, wondering who was on the other side. "I'm here for a Gym battle!"

The voice didn't hesitate. *"Then please, help yourself."*

A shiny metal box stuck out of the Gym wall. Its top slid open. Inside lay a shiny collection of . . .

Ash gasped.

"They're all Gym badges!" Dawn exclaimed.

Piplup, her friendly blue Water-type Pokémon, chirped in surprise.

Ash couldn't believe it, either. "Just . . . *take* one?" he asked, shocked.

The robotic voice explained. *"At the Sunyshore Gym, we skip the battling and give challengers a badge."*

"Skip the *battle?*" It was the craziest thing Ash had ever heard.

"Please, help yourself."

"Man!" Ash groaned in disappointment. This wasn't working out exactly as he'd hoped.

Dawn tried to make the best of it. "Might as well take one if they're giving them away," she suggested.

There was no way Ash would do something like that. "You've got to earn it!" he told her. "And that's *after* you win the battle, right, Brock?"

"Of course," Brock agreed. "Otherwise, what's the point of having Gyms?"

Dawn wondered how she could help her friend. Suddenly, she remembered something.

Not long ago, they had heard something about the Sunyshore Gym. Something bad.

"What did Paul say?" she asked herself, trying to remember. Paul was a Trainer from Veilstone City. When he heard they were heading toward Sunyshore Gym, he hadn't been happy. But what had he said? Dawn closed her eyes, thinking.

She remembered!

"That Gym is *not* legit," he had said angrily.

"This must've been what Paul meant," Dawn realized. It looked like Paul was right.

Ash wouldn't stand for it. "I want to see Volkner *now*!" he shouted into the speaker. "I wanna challenge that guy to a real Gym battle!"

"*That is not possible,*" the voice informed him. As Ash got angrier, it stayed perfectly calm and polite. Like it really was just a machine.

Ash ignored it.

He pounded his fist against the steel doors as hard as he could. "Volkner!" he yelled. "C'mon, I know you're in there! Hey! I came here to challenge you to a Gym battle, and I'm not leaving until that's what I get."

Nothing happened. Ash banged harder. "I want a Gym battle! *Volkner*!"

The doors shook and shuddered. But they didn't open.

"Please stop," the voice said. *"You must leave the premises at once. Please stop."*

"I want a Gym BATTLE!" Ash screamed, throwing his body against the door.

"Intruder," the voice announced, *"you will now be escorted off the premises by force. You will now be escorted off the premises by force. You will now be escorted off the premises by force."*

Dawn and Brock gaped as two slots above the doors slid open. Long metal arms shot out. There was a giant metal hand attached to each one. The hands grabbed Ash and lifted him off the ground.

Ash struggled against their tight metal grip. But they wouldn't yield.

"You will now be escorted off the premises by force," the voice repeated. Ash shouted for help, but there was nothing his friends could do.

He tugged at the metal hands. "Hey! Come

on, let me go! Let *gooooo!*"

"Use Mach Punch!" someone shouted from below.

Ash twisted around to see who had called out. But all he saw was a giant, furry Fire-and-Fighting-type Pokémon with a cloud of flame spurting out of its head. It was an Infernape.

And it was headed straight for him.

Chapter 3

Ash was trapped. The metal hands held him tight as Infernape lunged toward him. There was no escape. Ash squeezed his eyes shut and braced himself.

The Fire-and-Fighting-type Pokémon unleashed a massive Mach Punch.

The metal hands exploded in a shower of screws and gears. Ash flew into the air and landed on the ground with a loud thump.

"Infernape?" he asked in a daze. Where had the Pokémon come from? And why had it helped him?

"Good!" a man's voice said.

Ash looked up at the stranger who had come to his rescue. The man's yellow shirt and orange hair were as bright as the sun. He looked very proud of himself . . . and very familiar.

Brock's eyes widened. "Wait a minute—aren't you, uh. . . ?"

"I'm Flint from the Elite Four," the man said in a friendly voice. "Hey there!"

Ash couldn't believe it. "The Elite Four?" That meant Flint was one of the toughest Trainers in the entire Sinnoh region!

Flint grinned. "I'll say this—you're determined. Follow me. I'll bring you to Volkner."

Ash, Brock, and Dawn looked at one another in shock. This day was getting stranger by the minute.

"Volkner and I are good buds," Flint explained. "At the moment, he's over there." The famous Pokémon Trainer pointed at the looming glass Tower.

So they followed Flint to Sunyshore Tower.

The building was even more amazing from the inside. A see-through glass elevator carried them up to Volkner. As they rose toward the top of the Tower, the city shrank beneath them.

"Sunyshore City generates electricity from solar panels located all over town," Flint said. He pointed at the shining glass panels dotting every rooftop. "And every one of them is controlled from Sunyshore Tower."

"Whoa," Ash breathed. He had never seen anything like it.

Flint nodded. "Volkner's responsible for building this from the ground up!"

Ash was amazed. "Wow, Volkner built *this*?"

Finally, the elevator reached the top floor. The doors slid open, and they stepped onto a windowed observation deck. Ash and his friends pressed themselves against the windows, soaking in the view. The sparkling city was stretched out beneath them. It looked even more beautiful from above.

But they were jolted out of the moment by a sizzling crackle of electricity. They whirled around.

"It's a Raichu!" Ash exclaimed.

The stubby, orange Electric-type Pokémon was

surrounded by a halo of sparks. Ash, Dawn, and Brock backed away. But Flint took a step *toward* the Pokémon.

"Hey there," he said cheerfully.

"Flint, look out!" Ash warned him. Raichu evolved from Pikachu, and it was incredibly powerful.

Raichu lunged at Flint, who opened his arms wide.

Ash's jaw dropped open.

Raichu was giving Flint a hug!

Flint hugged it right back. "You look great, Raichu! Where's your partner?"

Before Raichu could respond, a pale young man appeared at the other end of the room.

"Hey! Volkner!" Flint said in his booming voice.

"Hey, Flint," Volkner said quietly. "Who are the kids?" But even though he'd asked the question, he sounded like he didn't care about the answer.

Volkner and Flint couldn't have been more different. Everything about Flint was bright—his smile, his voice, even his hair. Everything about Volkner was . . . faded. His pale hair hung limp. His mouth curved down, as if he didn't have the energy to smile. When he spoke, it sounded like talking made him want to take a nap.

"You've got a Gym battle challenger!" Flint said.

Ash couldn't imagine Volkner having enough energy for a handshake, much less a battle. But he introduced himself anyway. "Hi, nice to meet you. I'm Ash. I want a Gym battle!"

Volkner shrugged. "You saw the badges at the Gym. Just take one of those."

"No *way*!" Ash had never met a Gym Leader who acted like this. It just wasn't *right*. "I wanna earn my badge by *winning* the Gym battle. So please, let me challenge you to a battle."

Volkner glared at him. "Don't make me tell you again."

Ash didn't get it. "But why won't you—"

Volkner turned his back on Ash. "I've completely lost interest in battling."

Ash tried to imagine himself losing interest in battling. Not possible! "B-but . . ."

"Volkner, I can tell you Ash is an electrifying Trainer!" Flint said with enthusiasm. "And I'm sure if you just gave him a chance . . ."

Flint trailed off when he realized Volkner wasn't listening. The Gym Leader had turned away. He stared blindly out the observation window.

"What a day," Volkner murmured. "Beautiful. I'd like you to leave."

"Volkner!" Flint exclaimed. How could his old

friend be so rude? He searched for the words to convince Volkner to battle.

But before he could say anything, the Gym Leader slipped through another set of automatic double doors.

Just as suddenly as he had appeared, he was gone.

Chapter 4

Flint felt terrible about the way Volkner had treated Ash and his friends. To make it up to them, he took them to a cozy restaurant at the heart of Sunyshore City. The house specialty was a sweet, refreshing beverage.

"It's my treat," Flint said, as they all got a mug. "Drink up, folks!"

"Thanks so much, Flint!" Dawn and Brock said. They each took a big gulp.

"Wow! What a fantastic deep and rich flavor," Brock said.

"And what an aroma!" Dawn added.

But Ash just stared at the table. He couldn't stop thinking about Volkner.

The restaurant proprietor came toward them with a tray of sandwiches. He saw how much

Dawn and Brock were enjoying their drinks. "I'm happy you feel that way!" he told them, placing the tray on the table. "And this is all on the house."

"Oh, yum!" Dawn exclaimed. She was starving.

"That's wonderful, thank you," Flint said.

"Thank you, sir," Brock and Dawn added quickly. They eagerly grabbed a couple of sandwiches. But Ash didn't move.

"Why aren't you eating, Ash?" Dawn asked.

Ash didn't hear her. He just kept hearing Volkner's voice in his head.

I've completely lost interest in battling.

Over and over, until Ash couldn't take it anymore. He leaped out of his seat. "Okay, look, Flint. I can't go along with this! When I heard Volkner was the strongest Gym Leader, well, see, I got totally fired up. But I just can't believe how *un*-into battling Volkner is now!"

Flint couldn't argue. "Yeah," he said sadly. "Believe me. He wasn't always like this."

The proprietor nodded. "Right. Everybody

used to refer to Volkner as 'The Shining, Shocking Star.'"

"You're kidding!" Ash tried to picture Volkner shining or shocking anyone. He couldn't do it.

"He reminded everyone of a bolt of lightning!" Flint boasted. "Electrifying." Flint gazed into the distance, like he was seeing Volkner the way he used to be. "Back when I was a kid, this city was full of hoodlums—but Chimchar and I fought our way right to the top."

Flint told them about how Sunyshore City used to be. It had been a dark and grimy place, filled with danger. Roving gangs of punks preyed on the weak. Flint did his best to fight them off. But he was very young, and very alone.

"Then one day, I met Volkner," Flint told them, with a faint smile. "Suddenly, as if it were fated, we had a battle!"

Flint's Chimchar and Volkner's Pikachu had gone head to head. It had been very close. In the end, Flint won.

"But it wasn't long until Volkner challenged Chimchar and me once again," Flint continued.

"And this time, *Volkner* won. After that, we battled day in and day out to see who was the top Trainer in Sunyshore City."

"Wow!" Dawn could see that these memories meant a lot to Flint. "Did you guys battle that much because you didn't like each other?"

"No, no!" Flint protested. "That wasn't why."

The proprietor jumped in to explain. "Oh, Flint and Volkner were getting along. I think they both knew they'd always get along no matter what. It's knowing that fact that kept them going!"

"That changed when the two of us came across a rogue poacher deep in the forest," Flint said. "Facing an opponent together for the first time, we battled alongside each other! When it was over, even though we did manage to chase the poacher away, it took its toll. Truth is, we got beat up pretty badly."

Alone in the forest, they had lain in the mud, trying to get their strength back. Rain poured down on them, but they hadn't cared. They stared up at the sky, glad to be alive. And glad to have each other.

In the restaurant, Flint smiled, remembering how they both realized the truth at the same moment.

"It didn't matter if we got hurt," he explained. "Because after that day, we were good friends."

Ash just couldn't understand how *that* Volkner had turned into *this* one.

"But if Volkner's like what you say he is, why won't he battle me?" he asked.

"Is there something else?" Dawn added.

Flint hung his head.

The proprietor sighed unhappily. "I'll tell the rest of what happened," he said. "It was when Flint had just turned twenty. Volkner became the Gym Leader and stayed in Sunyshore City. And Flint, with a desire to gain greater strength and skills, went on the road—training in all conditions."

Ash glanced at Brock and Dawn. He tried to imagine what his journeys would have been like if he hadn't had his friends.

He guessed they would have been pretty lonely.

"Flint eventually became a member of the Elite Four," the proprietor said, "while Volkner started losing interest in battling the many Gym challengers who crossed his path. He was always into technology, and soon became obsessed with it. He built solar-powered systems all over the city, and Sunyshore Tower as well, which controls those systems. When finished, he could manage the entire city with solar-powered electricity! But after all was said and done, for some reason, Volkner felt like an empty shell."

The proprietor hesitated. "Something was missing from his life," he said quietly. "It's like everything had lost its meaning."

Flint shook his head. "I brought you to Volkner because I thought you could help him," he told Ash. "Your spark could make him feel like new!"

Suddenly, Volkner stepped out of the shadows in the back of the restaurant. "It was a wasted trip," he said flatly.

"Volkner!" Flint said, surprised to see his old friend. "How long have you been there?"

Volkner ignored him. He slumped onto a stool. "Give me the usual, please."

"Sure," the proprietor said. But he didn't sound happy about it.

"Volkner, you know how I feel about this," Flint said. He was getting upset. "Come on, snap out of it!"

Volkner sneered at him. "So, did you come back here just to give me a lecture, Mr. Elite Four?"

Fed up, Flint grabbed him by the collar and yanked him off the stool. "What'd you say?" he hissed.

Volkner went limp in his grip. "If you want to punch me, do it," he said. It was obvious he didn't care one way or another.

Flint was disgusted. He let go. "It's not even worth the time it takes to do it."

Volkner laughed.

That was more than Flint could take. He balled his hands into fists. "What's happened to you!" he shouted at his best friend. "What happened to the electrifying Volkner? 'The Shining, Shocking Star'!"

Volkner scowled. "Flint, we're not kids anymore. You've got to grow up sometime."

"Grow up?" Flint roared.

"Flint!" The proprietor stepped in between them. "Take a chance," he suggested. "Why don't *you* have that battle with Ash?"

"Battle with Ash?" Flint echoed. "Why would I do that?"

Ash thought this was the best idea he'd heard all day. "Come on, Flint!" he said eagerly. "Have a battle with me!"

"It's not every day one battles with a member

of the Elite Four, you know," Brock pointed out.

Dawn beamed. "I'd love to see that!"

"Volkner, you'll join us then, right?" the proprietor asked.

Volkner looked surprised by the question.

"After all, Flint's battling Ash in your place," the proprietor pointed out. "The least you could do is watch."

"Sure," Volkner said limply. "Whatever."

Flint sighed, wondering what had happened to his old friend. At least he had agreed to watch the battle. It wasn't much — but it was a start.

Chapter 5

Team Rocket didn't know anything about Sunyshore Gym or its leader—and they didn't care. When they looked at the Gym, all they saw was an opportunity to poach some Pokémon. They just had to figure out how.

"The Sunyshore Gym," James said, staring up at the imposing building. "Fetching!"

"So how do we go about fetching Pikachu?" Jessie asked.

Meowth had a surefire plan. "Piece a' cake—I say we *dig*!"

"That's *our* kind of gig," Jessie and James said together. They whipped out their shovels. But as James raised his shovel, something fell out of his pocket. It was a small, round piece of metal.

"James, you're shedding," Meowth said.

James gasped when he saw the metal rolling away. "My bottle cap! The rarest of the rare!" He lunged for the precious treasure — but not quickly enough. A funny-looking little machine wheeled over to the bottle cap.

"Trash identified," the machine said in a robotic voice. *"Disposing."*

"That's not trash, that's *treasure*!" James screamed, as the machine scooped up the bottle cap and rolled away. "You robotic *brute*!"

James flung his shovel to the ground. He raced after the cleaning machine. Jessie and Meowth had no choice. They followed him. It looked like their Pokémon-poaching plan would have to wait.

Inside the Gym, Team Rocket was the last thing on Ash's mind. He was completely focused on the upcoming battle. He stood at one end of the arena. Flint stood at the other. They stared at each other, their muscles tense, their nerves steady. They were ready to go.

"Attention!" announced the mechanical referee in its robot voice. *"The three-on-three Pokémon battle between Flint of the Elite Four and Ash from Pallet Town will now get under way!"* The referee waved a flag—the official start of the battle. *"And, begin!"*

"Ready or not!" Flint called. He tossed out a Poké Ball. Infernape burst out.

"So Flint's using Infernape," Ash said to himself. "Okay . . . Buizel, I choose *you!*"

He threw out a Poké Ball and Buizel popped out of it, ready for battle.

Up in the bleachers, Dawn leaned forward in her seat. There was space for an audience of hundreds, but today only Dawn, Brock, Volkner, and the proprietor were watching. It meant they had a perfect view of Ash's every move. "Flint's using a Fire-type, so Ash's got the advantage using Buizel, which is a Water-type," Dawn observed.

"Right!" Brock agreed. "When it comes to type advantage, Buizel's moves are super-effective on Infernape and not very effective the other way around!"

A few seats away, the restaurant proprietor sat with Volkner. The Gym Leader already looked bored.

"Well, well, it's been a while since you've seen Flint in a battle, isn't that right?" the proprietor asked him.

Volkner shrugged. "I really don't care."

Down in the arena, Buizel and Infernape faced off, sizing each other up. It was time for someone to make a move.

"Buizel!" Ash shouted. "Water Gun, let's *go*!"

It was one of Buizel's strongest attacks. The

sleek orange Pokémon shot a powerful plume of water directly at Infernape.

"Dodge it, quick!" Flint ordered.

Infernape leaped several feet in the air. The Water Gun attack didn't even touch it.

"Now use Ice Punch!" Ash shouted.

Buizel launched itself into the air. It came face to face with Infernape. The Water-type Pokémon was much smaller, but just as tough. Its arm heated up with a blue glow as it collected energy for its Ice Punch.

"Block that move!" Flint called.

Buizel slammed the Ice Punch into Infernape's fiery face, but Infernape crossed its arms and shielded itself from the blast.

Ash was impressed. This Infernape was fast *and* tough. But he wasn't about to back down. "Buizel, SonicBoom!"

"Smash it, Infernape!" Flint ordered.

The Fire-and-Fighting-type Pokémon smashed its massive fists into Buizel's SonicBoom waves, protecting itself from the attack.

"Use Aqua Jet!" Ash suggested.

A powerful gush of water rocketed Buizel straight toward Infernape.

"Now, Flare Blitz!" Flint shouted, just in time.

Infernape met the flood of water with a wall of flame. The Flare Blitz attack blazed into Buizel. It flew backward and landed in a heap.

"Buizel!" Ash cried in alarm.

The Water-type Pokémon was down for the count. That Infernape packed a punch! Ash gently lifted his dazed Pokémon off the ground.

"Buizel is unable to battle," the referee mech announced. *"The winner is Infernape."*

Dawn gasped. "Buizel was beaten in one move?"

"I guess type advantage doesn't mean a thing in Infernape's case," Brock said. He was impressed. This battle was going to be even tougher than they'd expected.

The proprietor nudged Volkner with his elbow. "Impressive, eh?"

Volkner sighed. "No, it's typical. I've seen it all before. I've fought countless weak challengers, and they're all confident at first."

But Ash was *still* confident. "Thanks, Buizel," he told his battered Pokémon. "Return." He paused for a moment, trying to decide which Pokémon to choose next. If he wanted to win this battle, he had to be more than strong. He had to be *smart*. "All right, Infernape, I choose *you*!"

"Whoa," Dawn said, as Ash's Infernape burst out of its Poké Ball. "Infernape versus Infernape!"

Brock was psyched. This battle was heating up. "A battle of the Fire-types!"

Ash didn't hesitate. "Infernape, use Flamethrower!"

His Infernape roared. Fire gushed out of its mouth and billowed toward Flint's Pokémon.

"Quick, smash it!" Flint said.

Flint's Infernape brought its fists together and slammed them down on the pillar of flame. It quickly flickered out.

"Flame Wheel, let's *go*!" Ash cried.

Ash's Infernape whirled itself into a spinning wheel of fire. It rolled across the arena toward Flint's Infernape.

"Knock it away!" Flint shouted.

Flint's Pokémon swept Ash's Infernape aside with a single mighty smack. Ash's Infernape went flying. But it shook itself off, ready for its next attack.

Ash was running out of options. "Use Mach Punch!" he commanded.

His Infernape charged Flint's Pokémon with a glowing fist. Flint's Pokémon easily deflected the blow. Ash's Infernape unleashed another Mach Punch, this one even more powerful than the first. But Flint's Infernape gracefully darted out of the way.

"I'll show you what a *real* Mach Punch looks like," Flint boasted. "Go!"

His Pokémon let loose an ear-shattering roar. It reared back, then lunged toward Ash's Infernape with the strongest Mach Punch Ash had ever seen. Ash's Pokémon hurtled backward. It dropped to the ground and didn't move.

"Infernape!" Ash rushed to his wounded Pokémon.

"Ash's Infernape is unable to battle," the referee

mech reported to the small crowd. *"The winner is Flint's Infernape!"*

"Just one move—*again*," Dawn said in a hushed voice.

"Flint's not in the Elite Four for nothing," Brock pointed out. Flint was one of the best Trainers he had ever seen. Ash was putting up a great fight. But Brock was afraid his time was running out.

"Great job, Infernape," Ash told his exhausted Pokémon. "Take a long rest."

As Infernape returned to its Poké Ball, Volkner stood up. He was ready to leave.

"What's wrong, Volkner?" Dawn asked.

"Hold it," the proprietor urged him.

Volkner shook them off. "I've seen enough."

"You should watch this until the end!" the proprietor insisted.

"It's a waste of time," Volkner argued.

"Oh, I see," the proprietor said sadly. "So you've completely lost touch with your feelings. You *must* have if you can't sense Ash's spark."

Volkner glanced down at Ash. He had one

Pokémon left to battle with, and he chose . . . Pikachu!

"I *thought* he'd use Pikachu for the last round," Dawn said.

Brock was worried. "Yeah, but for Ash, this is do or die, while Flint's only used Infernape the whole time."

Still, Pikachu was one of the most fearless and determined Pokémon they had ever met. If anyone could beat Flint's Infernape, it would be Pikachu.

"Pikachu, Quick Attack, let's go!" Ash cried.

Pikachu zipped through the air like a bolt of lightning. It slammed into Infernape. The Fire-and-Fighting-type Pokémon towered over the little yellow Electric-type Pokémon. But Pikachu's Quick Attack packed a lot of power.

Infernape took the blow full on. It barely reacted.

"Say, Pikachu's been trained well!" Flint exclaimed. "Flare Blitz, now!"

Infernape unleashed Flare Blitz, but Pikachu blocked it with Volt Tackle. It launched itself at

Infernape. Infernape's column of flames collided with Pikachu's electric aura, and a huge explosion erupted.

"Pikachu, no!" Ash cried in alarm.

But when the smoke cleared, Pikachu was still standing.

"Awesome," Dawn said.

"Pikachu's amazing!" Brock said. He was in awe of Ash's loyal Pokémon. "Enduring Flare Blitz by using Volt Tackle. . . ."

It was a brilliant move. Ash and Pikachu worked so well together in battle, it was like they were one.

Volkner couldn't force himself to leave. His eyes were glued to the battle.

"Well?" the proprietor asked knowingly. "Feel anything now?"

Volkner didn't answer.

"Guess we can seriously mix it up, right, pal?" Flint said happily. "Mach Punch, let's go!"

Infernape leaped into the air, preparing the attack.

"Pikachu, Iron Tail!" Ash shouted quickly.

But the Mach Punch knocked Pikachu to the ground before it could finish its attack.

"Pikachu!" Ash cried.

The Pokémon struggled to its feet. It was unsteady, but it was upright. And it was determined to keep going.

"All right!" Ash cheered, proud of his Pokémon. "Keep it up!"

"Use Close Combat," Flint ordered.

Hanging in midair, Infernape gave Pikachu a mighty kick. Then it started pummeling Ash's Pokémon with powerful punches. One final blow sent Pikachu tumbling toward the ground.

"Pikachu, hang in there!" Ash urged it. "Use Thunderbolt, *quick*!"

As it was falling, Pikachu flipped over to face Infernape. It somehow mustered a giant Thunderbolt attack.

Flint gaped at the little Pokémon. "Pikachu using Thunderbolt while falling through the air?" *That* was a move he'd never seen before. "All right, use Flare Blitz, now!" he told Infernape.

A wall of fire swept toward Pikachu as it was

still struggling to get off the ground.

"Dodge it!" Ash told it.

But Pikachu couldn't escape in time. Infernape's Flare Blitz slammed right into it.

"Pikachu, you okay?" Ash asked worriedly.

"Pikachu!" the Pokémon reported. No way was it giving up the fight.

The proprietor leaned toward Volkner. "You may remember the same thing happened when you first fought alongside Flint," he whispered.

Volkner pretended to ignore him. But the proprietor was right. Volkner *did* remember. He remembered every detail of that day in the forest. The rain, the mud, the Houndoom charging toward them—and his Pikachu, bravely taking hit after hit. Never giving up.

The attacks were coming fast and furious. Pikachu launched Quick Attack. Infernape countered with Close Combat. Pikachu hit back with Thunderbolt. But Infernape dodged it and launched Flare Blitz. The blast of fire sent Pikachu flying—straight toward the wall at the end of the arena.

"I'm coming, *Pikachuuuu*!" Ash flung himself between Pikachu and the wall. The impact slammed him back, *hard*. Ash dropped to the ground.

Dawn screamed. "Ash, no!"

Ash didn't move.

Chapter 6

Ash slowly picked himself up and tried to shake off the pain. He didn't care about himself. He just cared about his Pokémon. "Pikachu, are you okay?"

Pikachu nodded weakly. Ash had saved Pikachu from the full impact of the attack. But it was still dazed from the blow.

"Man, I'm glad." Ash hugged Pikachu tight.

"You know, that looks an awful lot like you back in the day," the proprietor told Volkner.

Volkner didn't want to admit it, but the proprietor was right. The truth was, the proprietor had seen it for himself.

"I'd never seen a more electrifying team than you two," the proprietor said. "I stopped being a poacher after that day—after all, that was the most electrifying battling I had ever seen! So, Volkner, I'd say you still have some unfinished Gym Leader business to take care of, don't you think?"

But Volkner was still lost in his memories. That day in the forest, the poacher's Houndoom had sent Pikachu flying—straight into a tree. Volkner had thrown himself in between Pikachu and the sturdy trunk. Like Ash, he would have done anything to save his Pokémon. And even after that blow, his Pikachu had been determined to fight on.

Just like Ash's Pikachu.

Volkner couldn't believe it. The battle was continuing!

Pikachu released a powerful Volt Tackle. Infernape hit back with its trusty Mach Punch. But Pikachu dodged the blow and launched *another* Volt Tackle. Infernape met it with Mach Punch. Its fist slammed into Pikachu, and the attack was almost too much for Ash's Pokémon to take.

"Pikachu!" Ash cried.

Volkner blinked. Suddenly, he could hear his own voice, echoing through time. He could almost see his young self, fighting side by side with Ash.

"I know you can do it, Pikachu!" Ash said.

Volkner was listening intently. Hadn't he said that exact thing himself, all those years ago?

He felt like deep inside him, something was waking up. Something that had been asleep for a very long time.

Ash urged Pikachu to use another Volt

Tackle, and another. Infernape countered with ThunderPunch. The attack collided with Volt Tackle. There was a huge explosion of smoke. It slowly faded away, revealing Pikachu, still on its feet!

For a moment, it looked like the battle would continue.

And then Pikachu wobbled.

It lurched forward.

It teetered backward.

It dropped to the ground.

It was done.

Ash rushed to Pikachu's side and gathered the Pokémon into his arms.

"Pikachu is unable to battle," the referee mech announced. *"Infernape is the winner! And the victory goes to Flint, of the Elite Four!"*

Ash didn't care about losing. He was just worried about his Pokémon. "Pikachu, hang in there," he urged it.

But Pikachu was okay. It had fought long and hard, and now it just needed a long rest.

"You battled hard," Ash said. "Thank you."

"It was a great battle!" Brock said, congratulating his friend. Even though Ash had lost, he had put up an amazing fight.

"You battled a member of the Elite Four!" Dawn said, sounding awed.

"Thanks," Ash said. He was proud of his Pokémon for how hard they had battled. He was also proud of himself. Maybe he had lost this time, but there was always a next time. And next time, he would *win*. "We're gonna work hard and get stronger than *ever*, right?"

Pikachu cheered weakly.

Volkner joined the others on the floor of the arena. He looked different than before. Somehow, he looked more . . . *alive*.

"Looks like I still have some unfinished business after all," he said. There was a new fire in his eyes. "A Gym Leader's job is to make sure every bit of that spark is passed along to all challengers!"

Flint beamed at his old friend. "Volkner! You mean it?"

For the first time in a very long time, Volkner

smiled. "Thanks to you and the proprietor—you finally made me realize that."

"I think *Ash* is the one who you should be thanking," the proprietor said.

Volkner agreed. "You were brilliant, Ash! All of your spark, and that of your Pokémon . . . watching you battle inspired me more than I can say."

Ash couldn't believe how much Volkner had changed. "Thanks! Does that mean you'll have a Gym battle with me?"

"Yes!" Volkner said. "An electrifying one, too."

"Oh, Ash!" Dawn exclaimed. She was thrilled for her friend. Finally, Ash would get the chance to win a new Gym badge.

"That's awesome!" Brock cheered.

"Yeah! I can't wait!" Ash pumped his fist in the air. As soon as his Pokémon were recovered, he would face Volkner in battle. And this time, he promised himself, he would win.

Over on the other side of town, Team Rocket had other plans.

Or at least, two of them did. James was still sobbing over his lost bottle cap.

"Yo, James, keep it up and you're going to dehydrate!" Meowth warned him.

"Get off it!" James wailed in sorrow. "You'll never know the pain such loss can bring."

Jessie rolled her eyes. They had more important things to worry about than bottle caps. "Focus your mind on this city," she urged him. "Solar power runs the whole show!"

Meowth pointed up at Sunyshore Tower. "Yeah, and on top of that little fun fact, Sunyshore Tower *runs* the whole show! Imagine if we made that baby our happy home."

Jessie's face lit up at the thought of it. "We'd climb the ladder to Sinnoh success so fast our heads would spin."

Even James perked up. "Win-*win*!" he cried. "Revenge will be sweet for stealing my bottle cap. The Tower is *mine*."

"Whoa." Jessie had never seen anyone get so upset over a bottle cap.

Meowth shrugged. "Lame logic, but it works!"

Meowth was right. Their motives didn't matter. The only thing that mattered was taking control of Sunyshore Tower.

And then using it to take control of everything else.

Chapter 7

"The battle between Ash, the challenger, and Volkner, the Gym Leader, will now get under way!" the referee robot announced.

Ash drew in a deep breath. He knew that challenging Volkner might lead to one of the toughest battles he had ever faced.

"Each side may use three Pokémon, and the match will be over when all three of either side's Pokémon are unable to battle!" the referee continued. "In addition, only the challenger will be allowed to substitute Pokémon."

"Just think," Ash told Pikachu, "if I win this battle, we're in the Sinnoh League! You ready, Pikachu?"

Pikachu cheered. It was ready.

The referee waved its flag. "And, begin!"

Volkner didn't hesitate. "Go, Luxray!" he shouted. A wide smile stretched across his face. His eyes sparkled. He looked like he had been born to battle.

His Luxray was just as eager. The Electric-type Pokémon was the final evolved form of Shinx. Its fierce eyes were trained on Ash.

"Grotle, I choose you!" Ash shouted.

Grotle burst out of its Poké Ball. The two Pokémon growled at each other, waiting to strike.

"So that means Ash's putting his Grass-type Grotle up against Volkner's Electric-type Luxray," Brock said, up in the bleachers. "It looks like a clear case of matching by type."

"Yeah, but Volkner's strong," Flint pointed out. "I just don't think type is going to be all that important. I'm so psyched!"

Dawn was glad that Volkner had found his spark again, but she was still rooting for her friend to win. "Ash, come on and show him what you've got!"

"All right, Grotle, use Razor Leaf!" Ash said.

The burly green Grass-type Pokémon shot a shower of sharp leaves in all directions.

"Luxray, dodge and use Spark!" Volkner called out.

The black Electric-type Pokémon danced away from Grotle's attack. It zapped a blinding blue spark straight into Grotle.

Ash flinched—that one looked like it hurt!

"Oh, wow!" Brock exclaimed. "That was some Spark."

But Grotle was a tough Pokémon with a thick,

sturdy shell. In only a moment, it was back on its feet.

"It sure was," Dawn admitted. "But I guess it was not very effective!"

Flint had faith in his old friend. "Just wait—see, Volkner's only beginning to get warmed up!"

"All right, Ash," Volkner said. His eyes were fixed on his opponent. "Your next move?"

Well, I knew it wasn't gonna be easy, Ash thought. He couldn't think about winning or losing. He had to just focus on the next attack, and the next. "So we'll just work harder!" he said out loud, suddenly cheerful. That was the great thing about Pokémon battles: The tougher they got, the more fun they were. "All right, Grotle, let's show 'em what we can do!"

Grotle growled in agreement. But before Ash could order an attack, something strange happened.

The lights went out!

At the same moment, the referee robot powered down. It toppled over on its side.

"What happened to the lights?" Dawn asked,

confused. She could barely see anything in the dark arena.

"What's going on, Volkner?" Ash called. "That's weird."

"Not sure." Volkner sounded worried. "Guess we're going to have to put our battle on hold until I figure this out!"

Volkner rushed over to the fuse box on the side of the arena. He fiddled with the switches and wires. But no matter what he did, the building stayed dark.

"Come on," Flint urged him. "Don't keep us waiting at a time like this!"

"I'm doing all I can," Volkner said, frustrated. Finally, he gave up and shut the fuse box. "It looks like the Gym's been left completely without power!"

Volkner thought he might be able to fix the power from outside. There was just one problem: The automatic doors were powered down, too. They were stuck inside!

Flint and Volkner managed to wedge their fingers into the crack between the doors.

They gave a mighty heave. The doors separated—but only a few inches. They were going to have to work much harder if they wanted to get out.

The two old friends had faced tougher battles than this. They could do it . . . together.

Flint counted down. "One . . . two . . . *GO!*"

At the same moment, they shoved the doors as hard as they could. Slowly but surely, the steel doors separated. They were free!

Flint rubbed his sore arm muscles. "Automatic doors are a pain when they're not automatic," he complained.

Volkner was about to agree. But he was distracted by the arrival of Officer Jenny. She rushed up to him, panic in her eyes.

"Volkner, we've got problems!" she cried.

Brock cried, too—but it was a cry of love.

"Wowwww!" he squealed. "Officer Jenny."

Suddenly, Brock forgot about the power problems. He forgot about everything but the beautiful Officer Jenny. He dropped to his knees and slapped one hand over his heart. He grabbed

Officer Jenny's hand with his free hand, and wrapped his fingers around hers.

"I could *never* be without power when I gaze into your eyes," he swore. "It's like—*aaaah!*"

Brock's faithful Croagunk had snuck up behind him and jabbed him before he could embarrass himself any further. (Croagunk had to do that a *lot*.)

"It's like . . . the opposite of this," Brock moaned, as Croagunk dragged him away.

Once Brock was out of the way, Officer Jenny could get down to business. "I regret to inform you that all the power in Sunyshore City has been cut off!"

Flint's jaw dropped. Things like this weren't supposed to happen in Sunyshore City. "That's *awful*."

Awful, but true. The city was completely still. The moving sidewalks had stopped moving. The cleaning and traffic robots had toppled over, useless. Confused and helpless, the citizens of Sunyshore City stood stock still in the streets.

"The thing is, Sunyshore City is run entirely

on solar power," Volkner said, thinking out loud. "The solar panels, positioned everywhere, collect the sun's energy and send it to Sunyshore Tower, which then functions as a power plant for the entire city. So *that* means something must have happened at Sunyshore Tower! I'll investigate."

But before he could, the ground began to shake.

"Look, the Tower!" Dawn cried. She pointed at the tall glass building. It was shaking. Smoke billowed from its base. They ran toward it to get a better look.

"All right, what's going on here?" Flint shouted.

A voice boomed out from the top of the Tower.

A *familiar* voice.

"Listen to the wisdom from the top of the Tower!" a girl shouted.

Ash frowned. He recognized the voice. It was *Jessie*, from Team Rocket. Causing trouble, as usual.

"Our diabolical plan is beginning to flower!" James shouted down.

James, Jessie, and Meowth appeared on the observation ledge at the very top of the Tower.

"On the wind!" Jessie cried.

"Past the stars!" James yelled.

"Fight the power!" Meowth added.

Jessie pointed toward the east side of the city. "There's no electricity over there."

James pointed west. "And wouldn't you know? None over *there*!"

"A blackout by any other name's just as black!" Jessie said triumphantly.

"When it comes to chaos, we've got the knack!" James added.

"Jessie!"

"And James!"

"Meowth, that's a name!"

They were so proud of themselves, they began singing a little song. "Putting the do-gooders in their place!" Jessie sang out.

"We're Team Rocket," James chanted.

"In your face!" the three of them cheered together.

"Team Rocket!" Ash said in disgust. He couldn't

believe those three had gotten their hands on Sunyshore Tower. This was a total disaster.

"Team Rocket?" Volkner asked, confused.

"They're a group of thieves who steal other people's Pokémon," Brock explained.

"You *lose*!" Jessie shouted down. "Correction! Stealing Pokémon is not on our agenda today!"

"Nope!" James agreed. "Rather, our current goal is tackling much more of a *towering* task. And I *do* mean towering."

"I hope you heard that play on words," Meowth jeered. "'Cause when we take this Tower, you'll think we're the team of the hour!"

Take the Tower? This was even worse than anyone had thought. But Ash and his friends were confused. How could Team Rocket *take* the Tower?

Officer Jenny was fuming. "So, that would lead me to believe that you're the ones who cut the power to the city!"

Up in her perch, Jessie laughed. "You *were* listening. You can hear *and* think!"

"We're stealing this Tower of power and all

its perks," James boasted. "But we won't waste a watt, so don't waste your time worrying your twerpish heads!"

"'Cause this baby's headed for headquarters, stat!" Meowth concluded. "Gotta scat!"

It wasn't possible, Ash told himself.

But possible or not, the Tower started to move.

"Keep those Towers rolling . . . " Team Rocket sang, as the Tower rolled out of town. They had attached it to giant wheels!

Ash made a fist. "They burn me up!"

But mad as Ash was, Volkner was even madder. After all, this was *his* town, and *his* Tower. "I will *not* let my Tower wind up in the hands of criminals like them!" he vowed. "Raichu, let's *go!*"

Volkner and his Electric-type Pokémon raced after the rolling Tower.

"I'm coming, too!" Flint called after him.

He wasn't the only one. Ash, Brock, and Dawn began to run. They were determined to catch up with Team Rocket and the Tower.

But then what?

Team Rocket had turned the observation deck into a control room. They sat behind their steering wheels, guiding the Tower exactly where they needed it to go.

"Feeling good, looking *great*, and flying right," Jessie bragged. "Let's hightail it home to headquarters."

Meowth couldn't believe the plan was working so well. "And now that the Sunyshore Tower's going be known as the Team Rocket Tower, we'll finally have some practical power and real clout. Know what that means?"

James's face lit up at the thought. "Our floors will be so warm and toasty, the Boss will prefer to sleep here than at home in his own bed! And to satisfy his culinary urges, gourmet stoves to cook his latest creation."

"And a hot water bathtub heater to soak away the stress of the day!" Meowth added. "Guess what he'll say?" He closed his eyes, imagining the moment. "'Thanks to Meowth and friends, my relaxation's a no-brainer, and I'm using clean energy and saving the environment at the same time!'" Meowth grinned. "If our future was any brighter, we'd need shades, baby! And we all know what *that* means, now don't we, my peeps?"

They did. "Climb the ladder of success," Team Rocket sang out together. "Leave the twerps *behiiiiiind!*"

Ash and his friends had no idea what Team Rocket was planning. They just knew Jessie, James, and Meowth had to be stopped.

Raichu and Pikachu were the fastest, so they caught up with the Tower first. When they saw what Team Rocket had done, they stopped in shock.

A moment later, everyone else caught up. They stared up at the Tower in horror.

Volkner gasped. "It's a *rocket!*"

Team Rocket had attached giant engines to the base of the Tower. They were planning to fly it away!

"Energy absorbers, normal!" James reported, up in the control room. "Power supply, normal! All systems ready for take off, stat."

Meowth wrapped his paws around the

controls. "Okeydoke, it's time for the official countdown! T-minus ten . . . nine . . . eight . . . seven . . . six . . . five . . . four . . ."

Down below, the ground shook. The Tower shuddered and smoked as the engines roared.

"That rocket's going to take off!" Volkner yelled.

"Not if I've got anything to say about it!" Ash shouted. He started running toward the Tower. Volkner and Flint were right behind him.

As the rocket lifted off the ground, Flint took a running leap and threw himself at it. Volkner and Raichu jumped next. They clung tight to the slippery glass.

Ash didn't stop to think. "Come on, Pikachu," he shouted.

Dawn couldn't believe what he was about to do. "Ash, *nooo!*"

But Ash had to stop Team Rocket. So he jumped.

His arms wrapped around the Tower just as it blasted off. A powerful wind rushed past him. It felt like invisible hands were dragging him into the sky. But he gritted his teeth against the wind and held on tight.

Flint was just above Ash, Volkner just below. Despite the wind, they were climbing. Slowly but steadily, they inched toward the observation deck.

"Ash, are you okay?" Volkner called up to him.

"I'm fine!" Ash shouted back. The wind snatched the words right out of his mouth.

The ground disappeared beneath them. Soon Sunyshore City was nothing but a sparkling dot against the bright blue lagoon.

"Good!" Flint called. "Just make sure you keep mov-*innnnnnnng*!" Flint screamed as a gust of wind blasted him off the rocket. He tumbled through the air, falling fast.

"Flint, *noooo*!" Volkner yelled. Flint kept falling. Down, down, down he went.

"Flint!" Ash screamed as Flint plummeted toward the sea. Ash twisted around, trying to keep the other Trainer in sight. The powerful wind swept past him, and Ash's hand slipped its grip. He flailed wildly, searching for something to hold onto. But there was nothing to hold but air.

Ash was falling! He was so high up, he couldn't even see the ground.

But he'd get there all too soon.

Volkner grabbed Ash's hand. He held on tight.

Ash dangled in the sky. His heart thumped loudly. His hands were sweaty, and he could feel Volkner's grip slipping.

"I'm going to pull you up, Ash!" Volkner shouted.

There was nothing Ash could do but hold on, wait, and hope.

Volkner heaved. Ash felt like his arm was being ripped out of its socket. But slowly, he rose through the air. Finally, he was back on the Tower. He wrapped his arms around its smooth glass and took a deep breath. He was safe.

For now.

"Thanks, Volkner," Ash said, when he had caught his breath. Pikachu clung to his shoulder, relieved that its friend was all right. "That was close!"

"Yes, but you're okay now," Volkner told him.

Ash thought of Flint: Was *he* okay?

He *had* to be. But Ash couldn't worry about it now. They had to keep climbing toward the top of the Tower. They had to stop Team Rocket!

"Over there," Volkner said, as they approached a doorway near the top. "I'm sure that's the service entrance. I should know—I did build the thing, after all."

Volkner pried open the service door, and they slipped inside the Tower. It was a huge relief to be out of the wind. Ash's arms felt like they were about to fall off. But he couldn't let himself relax. They had a job to do.

"I sure hope Flint's okay," Ash murmured. He couldn't stop thinking about it.

"He's a big boy," Volkner assured him. "Don't worry." Volkner was tracing the wiring that ran along the wall. "It looks like they've some-how rigged it to control the Tower from the observatory—"

He broke off as the Tower dipped and shuddered, nearly throwing Ash and Volkner to the ground. They held tight to the wall and tried to steady themselves.

"Okay, looks like we've leveled out," Volkner said. But he kept holding on.

Up in the control room, Team Rocket didn't need to hold onto anything. Their ride was perfectly smooth.

"Pure genius!" James exclaimed, proud of his work. "No matter which tilt the Tower takes, our seating stays straight."

"Dig it!" Meowth stretched out in his chair. "We got a million ways to use the groovy juice this airborne baby packs."

Jessie decided this was their best plan yet. "Plenty of pure power, a clean machine, and a safe and sound strategy make a tip-top team!"

"A speed demon's dream!" they cheered together.

Many miles below, a head of bright orange hair popped out of the water. It was Flint!

"Man, that was awful!" he gasped, spitting out a mouthful of water.

"Flint!" Brock cried in relief. He was standing on the side of the lagoon, searching for the Trainer.

"Are you all right?" Dawn asked anxiously.

Flint swam toward shore. "Yeah, I'm fine."

Brock leaned down and hauled him out of the water. "That's great," he said. He and Dawn had been so worried when they saw someone fall from the Tower.

So Volkner and Ash were still up there. He just hoped they were okay.

There was nothing Brock could do to help his friends up in the sky. But there was plenty of work to be done down on the ground. Brock, Dawn, and Flint made their way to the Sunyshore City Pokémon Center to see if there was anything they could do.

The first person they encountered was Officer Jenny. They quickly filled her in on what was happening.

"What?" Officer Jenny exclaimed. "Volkner and Ash are in the Tower?!"

"Right," said Flint. "But if I know my buddy Volkner, he'll have that Tower back in no time."

Nurse Joy joined them. Brock let out a howl of joy.

"*Yaaaaay!*" he screamed, and fell to his knees. He grabbed her hand. "Nurse Joy! One look at you, and my power meter's on *ten*. You give me such a—*JOLT!*" He screamed, as Croagunk jabbed him again.

Brock collapsed to the ground. ". . . along with you-know-who," he moaned, as the dark blue Poison-and-Fighting-type dragged him away again.

Nurse Joy and Officer Jenny looked serious. They had a big problem. "Since the backup generator here at the Pokémon Center has broken down, we've been working nonstop to get it back online," Officer Jenny explained.

"Unfortunately, there are a lot of Pokémon here that need serious care," Nurse Joy said. "And they can't afford to be without it much longer! Which leaves us with only one thing to do."

"What's that, Joy?" Dawn asked. She would do *anything* to help the sick and wounded Pokémon.

"We use these!" Officer Jenny said. She led them to two stationary bicycles that had been hooked up to a giant generator. Behind each bike was a meter that measured the power it would generate.

"Got it!" Flint cheered. "*People* power. Great idea, I like it!" Without being asked, he climbed onboard one of the bikes. "You may not know this, but I used to be quite the cyclist back when! All *riiiiiight*."

Flint started pedaling like crazy. Behind him, the lights on the power meter rose and rose. "C'mon, Brock," he shouted, filled with energy. "Time to get with the program and grab a bike!"

Brock was still sore from getting jabbed. And it was a *long* time since he'd been on a bike. Still, the Pokémon needed his help. . . .

"Uh, sure," he said, and climbed carefully onto the other bike. He held on tight, like it was a wild Pokémon that might throw him to the ground.

"It would help to pedal," Flint suggested. Then he let out a banshee yell and pedaled even faster.

Brock told himself that if Flint could do it, *he* could do it. "All *riiiiiight*!" he yelled, even louder than Flint. He began to pedal.

Joy's face filled with happiness as the generator buzzed with power. "Wonderful, thank you both," she said. "Now, keep it up, boys."

While Joy and Dawn tended to the wounded Pokémon, Brock and Flint pedaled.

And pedaled.

And pedaled.

Until finally, Brock couldn't pedal anymore.

"Man, I'm so tired, I can hardly move my feet," he moaned, slowing down.

"That is unacceptable!" Flint snapped. "Now show me some guts!"

Brock panted and gasped. His lungs were about to explode. "I'm fresh out of guts."

Joy stood before him, her hands clasped. "Please, Brock. You can do it. I believe in you!"

Brock took one look at Joy's face and felt energy surging through him. For her, he could do *anything*. *"Riiiiiiight!"* he shouted, pedaling faster than ever. "Yes, I shall pedal, with every last ounce of strength I can muster up!"

"I like it!" Flint cried. "Blow the top off that meter, and don't stop pedaling until you do."

Brock told himself he would pedal forever if he had to.

But he *really* hoped he wouldn't have to.

Up in the rocket, Ash and Volkner were doing everything they could to take back the Tower. They crept through the dark hallways, searching for a way into the control room.

"Ash, I feel badly that our Gym battle was so rudely interrupted," Volkner said quietly, as they made their way through the Tower. "Please forgive me!"

"Hey, no problem," Ash said. "We've got to get the Tower back, so don't worry about it."

"Right!" Volkner agreed. "Our sunny shores must be protected."

"Is that where the name comes from?" Ash asked. He'd never thought about it before.

"You hit it right on the head," Volkner told him. "Sunyshore City is known for its bright sunlight. It's the perfect name for a perfect city."

It was all starting to make sense now. "So then, that must be why you built all the solar panels and Sunyshore Tower, right?"

"That's right!" Volkner smiled, thinking about

how much he loved his hometown. "The truth is Sunyshore Tower is what makes Sunyshore City—which is why I have to get it back!"

As he spoke, they reached a set of large double doors.

"We can get to the observatory through here," Volkner said. "Ready to charge?"

"Ready," Ash said.

They reached for the door—just as a metal cage dropped down from the ceiling, right on top of them.

They were trapped!

Chapter 10

Ash rattled the bars of the cage. They wouldn't give.

Jessie's voice came from a speaker in the ceiling. "Now, isn't that a shame," she taunted them. "We've been watching you loser types since you glommed on board!"

"But I regret to inform you you've glommed your last bout of glommage!" James added.

Ash wasn't about to let a cage stop him. "Quick, Pikachu, Thunderbolt!"

"Raichu, Thunder!" Volkner said.

The two Electric-type Pokémon aimed their attacks at the metal bars. Bolts of electricity shot into the cage bars—but the bars didn't break. Instead, the electricity traveled along the bars into a pipe in the ceiling and disappeared.

They heard Meowth laughing through the speaker. "We recycle every bit of bolts and jolts you can dish out!" he jeered. "You know what *that* means. Team Rocket's feeling keen and going green. What a scene!"

"No, you don't!" Ash said. This was like a battle. He just had to choose the right Pokémon for the job. He threw out a Poké Ball. "It's up to you, Gible! I choose *you*!"

Gible burst out of the Poké Ball. It was ready to help.

"Now, Gible, use Rock Smash," Ash ordered the blue Dragon-and-Ground-type.

Gible's Rock Smash attack blasted through the cage bars. It left a giant hole behind it. Ash and Volkner climbed right through.

"Hey, no fair!" Meowth complained. "We don't want to deal with a Pokémon with teething problems!"

"Gible, that was excellent," Volkner congratulated the Pokémon.

But Gible wasn't done. The Pokémon had strong jaws and an even stronger appetite. It blasted through the double doors and barreled into the control room. Then it started chomping on everything in sight.

Team Rocket couldn't stand to see their precious control room getting blown to bits.

"Chomp on your own rocket!" Meowth squealed.

"That's expensive, you twit!" James shouted, backing away from the enraged Gible.

"You have an eating disorder!" Jessie yelled.

But Gible had done its job. The control room was nearly in ruins.

"Gible, return," Ash said. "Team Rocket — time for you to return Sunyshore Tower!"

Team Rocket wasn't ready to give up. They retreated to high ground, perching on top of the control platform they'd just been using.

"Time to return *you*," Jessie shouted at Ash.

"There's nothing worse than a defective twerp!" James charged.

Both of them threw out Poké Balls. "Seviper, you're *on*," Jessie said.

"Carnivine, come out for the fight!" James

called. Then he screamed as Carnivine exploded out of its Poké Ball — and wrapped its vines around James's head. "Wrong again!" James shouted, squirming in Carnivine's tight grip. "Not out for the *bite*!"

Volkner took advantage of the confusion. "Raichu, use Thunder!"

"Pikachu, Thunderbolt, let's go!" Ash joined in.

The Electric-type Pokémon fired their sizzling attacks — but once again, their electricity was just sucked up by the rocket. Their attacks were *helping* Team Rocket!

Meowth cackled. "Hel-*lo*! When you truly go green, you recycle *everything*!"

"Seviper, use Poison Tail!" Jessie commanded.

James had finally gotten himself free of Carnivine. "Use Vine Whip!" he ordered his befuddled Grass-type Pokémon.

Team Rocket's Pokémon charged at Raichu and Pikachu. Their attacks hit the Electric-type Pokémon head-on. Ash and Volkner's Pokémon cried out and toppled backward.

"Pikachu, are you okay?" Ash cried.

Pikachu's eyes were closed. It didn't move.

Volkner shook his Pokémon. "Come on, Raichu, wake up."

"Guess they got *bored*," Meowth taunted.

Jessie took her shot. "Seviper, dear, use Bite!"

"Follow suit, Carnivine!" James added.

"Okay, Grotle," Ash said, tossing out a Poké Ball. "Block 'em both!"

Grotle burst out of its ball and threw itself in the path of the Bite attacks.

"Grotle, awesome!" Ash cried. "Next, follow up with Razor Leaf, let's *go*!"

But Grotle didn't release a Razor Leaf attack. Instead, it began to glow.

"Grotle?" Ash asked in wonder.

"Grotle's evolving!" Volkner whispered.

The glow was blinding. Light filled the room. When it faded away, Grotle was gone. It its place was an enormous green Grass-type Pokémon. Jagged spikes jutted out of its jaw. A tree sprouted from the giant shell on its back. Its red pupils glowed with fury.

"Torterra!" it shrieked, in a thundering voice. A funnel of green light blazed out of it and slammed into Seviper and Carnivine.

Volkner gaped. "Wow, Torterra used Leaf Storm!"

"Awesome!" Ash said. He was so proud of his Pokémon. "Torterra, that's so cool that you can use Leaf Storm!"

"Hey, time *out*!" Jessie whined, from her safe

perch. "Isn't sudden Evolution against all the rules?"

"If you twerps insist, the least you can do is use an Electric-type move so we can recycle it. Sheesh!" James moaned.

Meowth wasn't ready to retreat, no matter how powerful Torterra was. "We're all just getting warmed up. Up on your feet and *fight*," he urged the dazed Team Rocket Pokémon, sending them back into battle.

"Now, Torterra, use Leaf Storm!" Ash shouted.

Torterra let loose another blaze of green light. The attack was so powerful it blasted a hole in the side of the Tower—and blew Team Rocket straight through it!

"We're blasting off again!" they screamed, as they plummeted toward the ground.

"We did it, Volkner!" Ash cried, as he watched Team Rocket disappear into the distance.

But it wasn't quite time to celebrate. "There's still a small problem," Volkner pointed out. "We've got to get the Tower back to Sunyshore City."

The only question was: how?

Volkner thought hard. There had to be a way, and if there was, he had to find it.

Then, he had it. "We've still got their rocket, right?" he said, grinning. "Raichu, Pikachu—I need your help!"

Chapter 11

Back in Sunyshore City, Brock was fading fast. His feet had slowed on the pedals. His power meter had nearly dropped to zero.

He gasped for air. "I've never been this exhausted in my entire life!"

"Brock, we need more power," Dawn said urgently. "Come on, hang in there!"

"You don't understand," Brock moaned.

Nurse Joy was distressed. "Brock, please?"

A jolt went through Brock. And this time, it wasn't Croagunk, but the sound of Joy's voice.

"Do it for me?" she pleaded. "Can't you see I *need* you?"

Brock's eyes bulged. "You *need* me?" That was all he had to hear. "I'll bike until I burst those bars!" he shouted.

"Way to go!" Flint cheered, pedaling his heart out. "Keep it up."

Both their meters rose toward full power.

Suddenly, the windows began to rattle.

"Look at that!" Dawn said, pointing.

Joy glimpsed something hurtling through the sky. "Sunyshore Tower!" she cried.

"And it's headed right for us!" Dawn exclaimed.

They screamed in horror—but at the last moment, the Tower veered upward and cleared the building. It rocketed toward town center. As they sighed in relief, power returned to the Pokémon Center.

"It looks like they were able to fix the generator," Joy said happily. "Oh, thank goodness!"

No one was happier than Brock—he could finally stop pedaling. At least for the moment. The generator was just a temporary solution. Sunyshore City and its Pokémon wouldn't be safe until Ash and Volkner got the Tower back where it belonged.

They were trying. Up in the Tower, Raichu, Pikachu, and Luxray were aiming Electric-type attacks at the rocket's central power collector. The rocket absorbed their power — it was the only thing that kept them in the air.

"Keep it up, guys!" Ash urged them.

Volkner steered the rocket, carefully aiming for the right spot.

"We're passing over the Sunyshore Gym," he said. "Braking system, engage. Prepare to land!"

He pulled up hard on the thrusters, and the Tower shuddered beneath them. Pikachu stumbled. It nearly lost control of its attack.

"Volkner!" Ash cried in alarm.

"We're fine, Ash," Volkner assured him. "Please try and have a little faith in me. After all, remember I *did* build this Tower."

The Pokémon were tiring. But they wouldn't give up until the Tower was back where it belonged. They kept firing Electric-type attacks at the power collector. The rocket surged forward.

Volkner targeted the landing site. He rotated

the Tower until it pointed straight up into the air.

"Gooooo!" He engaged the engines and brought the rocket safely to the ground. They touched down with a thunderous thud. An enormous plume of smoke and dust erupted around them. Cracks splintered the walls of all the nearby buildings.

When it was all over, the Tower was on the ground, right where it belonged. The city was saved!

Ash and Volkner rejoined their friends in front of the Sunyshore Gym.

Brock's eyes widened when he saw Torterra. "Wow, so Grotle evolved?"

"Yup," Ash said proudly.

"Torterra . . ." Dawn activated her Pokédex to find out more about the new Pokémon.

"Torterra. The Continent Pokémon. Its large back and sedentary nature offer an ideal place for smaller Pokémon to build their nests."

Dawn smiled. "Nice to meet you, Torterra!"

Torterra gave her a friendly growl in return.

"As you can see, I'm going to need some time before we can have our battle," Volkner said, nodding at the cracks in the Gym walls. "But I'll let you know the minute I get things back in order around here."

"No problem!" Ash said. "And in the meantime, I'll be training hard for when you're ready to go."

Volkner grinned. "Good!"

There was plenty to keep them busy in the meantime. Dawn was planning to enter the Grand Festival. Brock was eager to observe the strange and interesting Pokémon of the Sinnoh region. And Ash had many more battles ahead of him.

Flint and Volkner waved good-bye. Ash could tell how happy they were to be together again, and he understood. He was excited to face whatever new adventures and challenges waited for him in Sinnoh. But he was even more excited to face them with his friends by his side. For just as Sunyshore City got its power from Sunyshore Tower, Ash, Brock, and Dawn got their power from one another.